# MASTER *English* THROUGH HINDI

ARUNIMA JUNEJA

First Published in May 2023

**ISBN:** 978-93-5741-436-4

**BLUEROSE PUBLISHERS**

www.BlueRoseONE.com

info@bluerosepublishers.com

+91 8882 898 898

**Cover Design:**

Muskan Sachdeva

**Typographic Design:**

Rohit

**Distributed by:** BlueRose, Amazon, Flipkart

# Contents

PART A – GRAMMER
(INTRODUCTION TO BASIC GRAMMER CONCEPTS)



PART B – INTRODUCTION TO STORY WRITING
(FROM HINDI TO ENGLISH)

PART C - INTRODUCTION TO
E-MAIL WRITING AND INFORMAL MESSAGE.



PART D – INTRODUCTION TO
EMAIL WRITING AND INFORMAL MESSAGE WRITING

# PART A

## GRAMMER
## (INTRODUCTION TO BASIC GRAMMER CONCEPTS)

# Noun/संज्ञा

हिंदी व्याकरण में Noun को संज्ञा भी कहते हैं। संज्ञा या Noun वाक्य संरचना में मदद करता है।

In Hindi grammer, Noun is also called as Sangya. The main purpose of Noun is to help structuring a sentence.

## Definition of Noun/संज्ञा

किसी भी व्यक्ति, स्थान और वस्तु के नाम को संज्ञा कहते हैं।

The name of person, place or thing is called as noun.

Example:-

Ram (राम)

Table (मेज)

Mumbai (मुंबई)

Let's have a look at the sentences containing Nouns. (चलिए वाक्य में संज्ञा को देखते हैं)

This Chair is new - ये कुर्सी नयी हैं।

Tina is a good girl - टीना अच्छी लड़की हैं।

Delhi is the capital of India - दिल्ली भारत की राजधानी हैं।

| Glossary | |
|---|---|
| व्यक्ति - person | कुर्सी - Chair |
| स्थान - place | नया/नयी - New |
| वस्तु - Thing | राजधानी - Capital |

## Types of Noun संज्ञा के भेद

1) Proper Noun (व्यक्तिवाचक संज्ञा)
2) Common Noun (जातिवाचक संज्ञा)
3) Collective Noun (समूहवाचक संज्ञा)
4) Material Noun (द्रववाचक संज्ञा)
5) Abstract Noun (भाव वाचक संज्ञा)

### 1. Proper Noun व्यक्तिवाचक संज्ञा

जो किसी भी व्यक्ति, स्थान या वस्तु का बोध कराता है, उसे व्यक्तिवाचक संज्ञा कहते हैं।

A Noun which belongs to a particular or individual name, person, place or thing is called as Proper Noun.

**For example:** Ram (राम), Taj Mahal (ताजमहल), Agra (आगरा)

**वाक्य/Sentences**

Ganga is a river - गंगा एक नदी है।
Meena is playing - मीना खेल रही है।
I live in New Delhi - मैं नई दिल्ली में रहती हूँ।

**Glossary:-**

River – नदी    Play – खेलना    Live – रहना

### 2. Common Noun जातिवाचक संज्ञा

वैसे नाम जिनमें जाति भर के बारे में बोध हो उसे जातिवाचक संज्ञा कहते हैं।

Common Nouns are the words which name the place, people, things etc, but they are not actual name of place, people or things.

For example

| Boy, | girl, | table, | chair |
|---|---|---|---|
| (लड़का) | (लड़की) | (मेज़) | (कुर्सी) |

**वाक्य / sentence**

Anil is an intelligent boy. - अनिल होशियार लड़का हैं।

Meena is a smart girl. - मीरा स्मार्ट लड़की है।

Animals live in forests. - जानवर जंगल में रहते हैं।

3. Collective Noun **समूहवाचक संज्ञा**

वैसी संज्ञा जो कि पूरे समूह या जाति के लिए इस्तेमाल हो उसे समूहवाचक संज्ञा कहते हैं।

A noun which is used for group collectively is known as collective noun.

For example

Herd (समूह)

Bunch (गुच्छा)

Crowd (भीड़)

| Glossary | | |
|---|---|---|
| Boy- लड़का | Chair - कुर्सी | Forest - जंगल |
| Girl- लड़की | Intelligent - होशियार | Herd - समूह |
| Table- मेज़ | Animals - जानवर | Bunch – गुच्छा<br>Crowd - भेड़ |

**वाक्य/Sentences of collective Noun**

Hari gave me bouquet of flowers - हरि नें मुझे फूलों का गुलदस्ता दिया।

I bought a dozen banana today - मैंने आज एक दर्ज़न केले खरीदे।

4. Material Noun **द्रववाचक संज्ञा**

वैसी संज्ञा जो कि तरल पदार्थ हो। जिसकी गिनती ना हों सके।

Nouns that refer to the names of liquid or material is called as Material Noun.

For example

| Gold, | Silver, | Water, | Sunlight |
|---|---|---|---|
| (सोना) | (चाँदी) | (पानी) | (सूर्य की रोशनी) |

**वाक्य/sentences**

The dentist placed a silver tooth in his mouth.

दांतो के डॉक्टर ने उसके मुँह में चाँदी का दाँत लगाया।

Gold is expensive - सोना महंगा है।

There is water in the glass - गिलास में पानी है।

| Glossary | |
|---|---|
| Bouquet - गुलदस्ता | Silver - चाँदी |
| Dozen - एक दर्जन | Water - पानी |
| Liquid - तरल | Sun - सूर्य |
| Count - गिनती | Sunlight - सूर्य की रोशनी |
| Gold - सोना | Dentist - दाँतो का डॉक्टर |
| | Tooth - दाँत |
| | Expensive - महंगा |
| | Glass - गिलास |

5. <u>Abstract Noun</u> **भाववाचक संज्ञा**

वह संज्ञा जिसका सिर्फ आभास होता है उसे भाववाचक संज्ञा कहते है।

The feelings or quality which can be felt are called as Abstract Noun.

**For example**

Honest - ईमानदार

Clever - चालाक

Beauty - सुन्दर

**वाक्य/Sentences**

Prerna is very intelligent - प्रेरणा बहुत होशियार है।

Ram is very kind - राम बहुत दयालु है।

Seema is very beautiful - सीमा बहुत सुन्दर है।

<u>Let's Recap</u>

| **शब्दकोष/Glossary** | | | |
|---|---|---|---|
| | अब तक Till how | | |
| 1. | Noun - संज्ञा | 24. | गिनती - Count |
| 2. | व्यक्ति - Person | 25. | सोना - Gold |
| 3. | कुर्सी - Chair | 26. | चांदी - Silver |
| 4. | स्थान - Place | 27. | पानी - Water |
| 5. | नया/नयी - New | 28. | सूर्य - Sun |
| 6. | राजधानी - Capital | 29. | सूर्य की रोशनी -Sunlight |
| 7. | अच्छा - Good | 30. | दांतो का डॉक्टर -Dentist |
| 8. | नदी - River | 31. | दाँत - Tooth/ Teeth |
| 9. | खेलना - Play | 32. | महंगा - Expensive |
| 10. | रहना - Live | 33. | गलास - Glass |

| 11. | लड़का - Boy | 34. | ईमानदार - Honest |
|---|---|---|---|
| 12. | लड़की - Girl | 35. | चालक - Clever |
| 13. | मेज - Table | 36. | सुंदर - Beautiful |
| 14. | कुर्सी - Chair | 37. | दयालु - Kind |
| 15. | होशियार - Intelligent | | |
| 16. | जानवर - Animals | | |
| 17. | जंगल - Forest | | |
| 18. | गुलदस्ता - Bouquet | | |
| 19. | गुच्छा - Bunch | | |
| 20. | भीड़ - Crowd | | |
| 21. | समूह - Herd | | |
| 22. | एक दर्जन - A dozen | | |
| 23. | तरल - Liquid | | |

# Pronoun/ सर्वनाम

हिंदी व्याकरण में Pronoun को सर्वनाम कहते हैं।

## Definition of Pronoun/सर्वनाम

A Pronoun is a word which is used in place of a Noun.
सर्वनाम वह शब्द है जो संज्ञा के स्थान पर प्रयोग किया जाता है।

**For example जैसे कि**

| English Pronoun | हिंदी |
|---|---|
| I | मैं |
| You | तुम, आप |
| He | वह (लड़के के लिए इस्तेमाल होता हैं) |
| She | वह (लड़की के लिए इस्तेमाल होता हैं) |
| We | हम |
| They | वे (एक से ज्यादा लोग) |
| Me | मुझे |
| Him | उसे |
| Her | उसकी |
| Us | हम |
| Them | उनको |
| My | मेरा, मेरी |
| Your | तुम्हारा/तुम्हारी/आपका/आपकी |
| His | उसके (लड़के के लिए) |
| Her | उसकी (लड़की के लिए) |
| Their | उनके |
| Mine | मेरा |

| | |
|---|---|
| Yours | तुम्हारा |
| Our | हमारा |
| Their | उनका |
| It | चीज के लिए इस्तेमाल होता हैं। |

Learn Pronoun so that we can use them.

सर्वनाम याद कीजिये ताकि हम उनका इस्तेमाल कर पायें।

# Linking Verbs/ संयोजन क्रिया

| Am | is | are | was | were |
|---|---|---|---|---|

Am - मैं हूँ - यह अपने आप के लिए इस्तेमाल होता हैं।

**For example जैसे कि**

I am a girl. - मैं एक लड़की हूँ।
जब भी हम अपनी बात करते हैं जैसे-
I am ten years old. - मैं दस साल की हूँ।
I am a good girl. - मैं एक अच्छी लड़की हूँ।

**But/पर**

जब हम ये बताते हैं कि हम क्या करते हैं या कहाँ रहते हैं तब हम am का प्रयोग नहीं करते

When we tell about ourselves like what we do or live then we don't use 'am'.

**Like**

I live in Mumbai. - मैं मुंबई में रहता हूँ। (✓)
I am live in Mumbai. - ये गलत हैं (x)
I study in 10th class. - मैं दसवीं कक्षा में पड़ता हूँ। (✓)
I am study in 10th class. – (x)
पर जब हम जो कर रहे हैं वो बताते हैं तो 'am' का प्रयोग होगा - जैसे कि

I am living in Mumbai.

I am studying in 10th class.

**Linking verb is**

It is used with one person like he and she. Please note that I and you also is used for one person but we don't use 'is' with 'I' and 'you' .

"Is" का मतलब होता हैं "हैं" - यह लड़की या एक लड़की के लिए इस्तेमाल होता हैं याँ एक चीज के लिए भी इस्तेमाल हों सकता हैं।

**For example जैसे कि**

He is a good student. - वह एक अच्छा विद्यार्थी है।

She is a good girl. - वह एक अच्छी लड़की है।

This is a ball. - वह एक बॉल है।

This is a chair. - वह एक कुर्सी है।

**Linking verb are**

"Are" linking verb is used with more than one person like they, we, Sonu and Meera.

"Are" एक से ज्यादा व्यक्तियों यां चीज़ो के लिए इस्तेमाल होता हैं।

**For example जैसे कि**

We are playing football.

हम फुटबॉल खेल रहे हैं।

They are going to the market.

वह मार्किट जा रहे हैं।

"Are" का इस्तेमाल you के साथ भी होता है।

जैसे कि - you are very nice - तुम बहुत अच्छे हो

"Are" का इस्तेमाल दो लोगों के साथ भी होता है जैसे कि –

Sonu & Monu are best friends.

सोनू और मोनू पक्के दोस्त हैं।

Meera & Mohan are playing baseball.

मीरा और मोहन बास्केट बॉल खेल रहे हैं।

## Linking verb was

'Was' is a linking verb which is used for person but for past.

'Was' एक व्यक्ति के साथ इस्तेमाल होता है पर यह भूतकाल के लिए इस्तेमाल होता है।

## For example / जैसे कि

She was tired.

वह थक चुकी थी।

He was very angry.

वह बहुत गुस्से में था।

I was very hurt.

मैं बहुत जख़्मी था।

Note "was" is not used with "you" though "you" denotes a single person.

## Linking verb were

Were दो या अधिक लोगों या वस्तुओं के साथ लगता है तथा वह भूतकाल के लिए इस्तेमाल होता है।

Were is used for two or more people or things and it represents the past.

<u>For example जैसे कि</u>

Ritu & Arnav were good friends.

रीतु और अरनव अच्छे दोस्त थे।

They were very helpful.

वह बहुत मददगार थे।

We were really enjoying.

हम बहुत मज़ा कर रहे थे।

Note: - "Were" is also used with "you" though "you" denotes single person.

नोट - "Were" "You" के साथ भी इस्तेमाल होता है जबकि "you" एक व्यक्ति के लिए इस्तेमाल होता है।

<u>Recap</u>

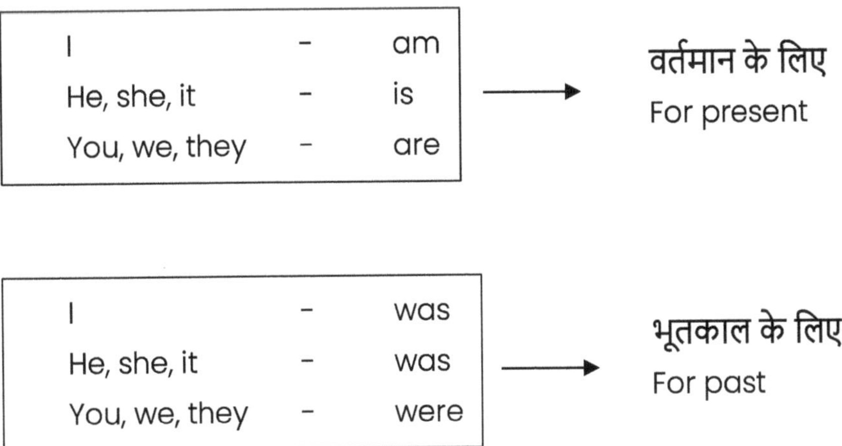

| | | |
|---|---|---|
| I | - | am |
| He, she, it | - | is |
| You, we, they | - | are |



| | | |
|---|---|---|
| I | - | was |
| He, she, it | - | was |
| You, we, they | - | were |

Glossary

| | | |
|---|---|---|
| विद्यार्थी | - | student |
| थकना | - | tired |
| गुस्सा | - | angry |
| जरूरी | - | hurt |
| मददगार | - | helpful |
| मजा | - | enjoy |

## Worksheet

### Use - is / am /are

1. I .............. a girl. (मैं एक लड़की हूँ)
2. You .............. very nice. (तुम बहुत अच्छी हो)
3. Hari .............. is a boy. (हरी अच्छा लड़का है।)
4. They.............. six girls. (वह छः लड़कियाँ हैं।)
5. We.............. very happy. (हम बहुत खुश हैं।)
6. This .............. a ball. (यह एक बॉल है)
7. These.............. two chairs. (ये दो कुर्सियाँ हैं।)
8. Sonu and Preeti.............. good friends. (सोनू और प्रीति अच्छे दोस्त हैं।)
9. Mini.............. very helpful. (मिनी बहुत मददगार है)
10. I............ five years old. (मैं पाँच साल का हूँ)
11. This book.............. very interesting. (यह किताब बहुत दिलचस्प है)
12. He.............. very tall. (वह बहुत लम्बा है)
13. They.............. reading a book. (वह किताब पड़ रहे हैं)
14. It.............. a big elephant. (यह बड़ा हाथी है)
15. The girls.............. going to the mall. (लड़कियाँ मॉल जा रही हैं)

| Glossary | | |
|---|---|---|
| अच्छी - nice | मददगार - helpful | मॉल - mall |
| खुश - happy | दिलचस्प - interesting | लम्बा - tall |
| कुर्सियाँ - chairs | पड़ना - read | |
| | बड़ा - big | |

## Worksheet

Fill with was / were

1. I.............. so happy yesterday.

   (मैं कल बहुत खुश थी)

2. You.............. very busy on Sunday.

   (तुम रविवार को बहुत व्यस्त थी)

3. Shanti & Monty.............. late for school yesterday.

   (शांति और मौटी कल स्कूल के लिए लेट थे)

4. She.............. in Delhi last month.

   (वह पिछले महीने दिल्ली में थी)

5. We.............. at school last Saturday.

   (वह पिछले शनिवार स्कूल में थे)

6. The boys.............. climbing the trees.

   (लड़के पेड़ो पर चड़ रहे थे)

7. He.............. swimming in the pool.

   (वह पूल में तैर रहा था)

8. The monkey..............eating a bananas.

   (बंदर केला खा रहा था)

9. The dog......... sleeping.

   (कुत्ता सो रहा था)

10. They.............. very rude.

    (वह बहुत असभ्य थे)

## Glossary

1. Yesterday - कल

2. Climb - चढ़ना

3. Swim - तैरना

4. Rude – असभ्य

# Helping Verbs/ सहायक क्रिया

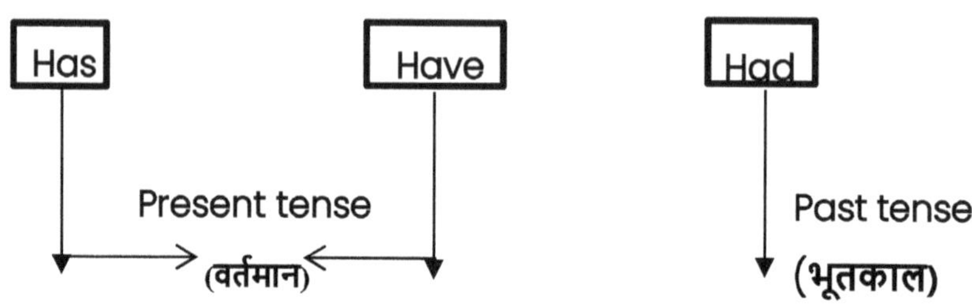


| Single person or things. (एक व्यक्ति या चीज़ के साथ लगता है) | For two or more person or things. (एक या ज्यादा लोगों या चीजों के साथ लगता है) | For one as well as two or more person. |
|---|---|---|
| Has/ Have/ Had | जब कोई वस्तु या समय किसी के पास होती है तो हम (has / have / has ) का इस्तेमाल करते हैं। When some thing or time or anything belongs to someone, so to represent that we use has/ have / had. It conveys the act of possession. | |
| Has | Is used for present and is used for one person. Has का इस्तेमाल वर्तमान के लिए और एक व्यक्ति के लिए होता है। | |
| Have | is a helping verb which is used for present and for more than one person. Have का इस्तेमाल वर्तमान के लिए होता है और एक से अधिक व्यक्ति के लिए। | |

| Had | is a helping verb which is used for past and is used for all (one person / more than one person). |
|---|---|

<u>For example **जैसे कि**</u>

| Has | Have | Had |
|---|---|---|
| 1.Sheetal has a red bottle.<br>(शीतल के पास लाल बोतल है) | 1.Sheetal and Raj have a red bottle.<br>(शीतल और राज के पास लाल बोतल है) | 1.Sheetal had a red bottle.<br>(शीतल के पास लाल बोतल थी)<br>Sheetal and Raj had red bottle.<br>(शीतल और राज के पास लाल बोतल थी ) |
| 2. He has many books.<br>(उसके पास बहुत किताबें है) | 2.They have many books.<br>(उनके पास बहुत किताबें हैं) | 2. He had many books.<br>(उसके पास बहुत किताबें थी)<br>They had many books.<br>(उनके पास बहुत किताबें थी) |

Has/ have/ had is also used for defining present perfect or past perfect which we will do later.

इन तीनों का इस्तेमाल चुका है या चुके थे में भी होता है, जो कि हम बाद में करेंगे।

**Note:** - I and you के साथ "have" लगता है जबकि वह एक व्यक्ति होते हैं।

## Worksheet

Has/have/had

1. They................ exam tomorrow. (कल उनका इम्तिहान है।)
2. An apple................ many seeds. (एक सेब में बहुत बीज होते हैं)
3. My brother................ many cars. (मेरे भाई के पास बहुत कारे हैं)
4. Dia................ long hair. (दीया के लंबे बाल हैं)
5. We................ a lot of fun yesterday. (हमनें कल बहुत मज़ा किया)
6. She................ a dog, but he died some days ago. (उनके पास एक कुत्ता था पर उसकी कुछ दिन पहले मृत्यु हो गयी है)
7. Do you................ a rough notebook? (क्या तुम्हारे पास कोई रफ़ कॉपी हैं)
8. I................ a beautiful pencil box. (मेरे पास सुंदर पेंसिल बॉक्स हैं)

जब हमें कहीं जाना होता है तो भी हम has/ have/ had का इस्तेमाल करते हैं। जैसे -

When we have to go somewhere then also we use helping verbs has / have / had.

For example जैसे कि

I have to go to school tomorrow.

(मुझे कल स्कूल जाना है)

She has to go to market.

(उसे मार्केट जाना है)

We had to go for picnic.

(हमें पिकनिक जाना था)

# Prepositions /संबंधसूचक अव्यय

Prepositions are the words that connect nouns, pronouns, & phrases to other words in a sentence.
वे शब्द या शब्दों का समूह जो किसी सर्वनाम या संज्ञा और वाक्य के भाग के बीच के संबंध को दर्शाते हैं। जिस संज्ञा या सर्वनाम इसका object (आबजेक्ट) कहलाता है।

For Example - **जैसे कि**

I am going to temple.
(मैं मंदिर जा रहा हूँ - object है - मंदिर/ temple)

The ball is on the table.
(बॉल टेबल पर है)

Let's now do all the prepositions

**चलिए अब** prepositions **करते हैं -**

**1.** From (से)

**(a)** use - **किसी जगह से**

(From some place)

1. They came from school.
   (वह स्कूल से आए थे)
2. I am coming from Delhi.
   (मैं दिल्ली से आ रहा हूँ)

**(b) किसी समय से**

1. I will work from tomorrow.

   (मैं कल से काम करूँगा)

2. He will join from Wednesday.

   (वह बुधवार से जाइन करेगा)

**(c) किसी स्रोत से**

(From any source)

1. I heard it from Seema.

   (मुझे सीमा से पता चला)

2. Sita saw the word meaning from the dictionary.

   (सीता ने शब्द का मतलब डिक्शनरी से देखा)

**2. In (में)**

**(a) use - जगह में**

1. I live in London.

   (मैं लंदन में रहता हूँ)

2. Dhruv is studying in America.

   (ध्रुव अमरीका में पड़ा रहा है)

**(b) किसी वस्तु में (के अंदर)**

1. My pen is lying in my pencil box.

   (मेरा पैन पैंसिल बाक्स में पड़ा है)

2. There is milk in the glass.

   (गलास में दूध है)

3. I read it in a book.

(मैंने एक किताब में पड़ा था)

**(c) समय में**

1. I came to Gurgaon in 2015.

(मैं गुडगाँव में 2015 को आया था)

2. She was born in January.

(वह जनवरी में पैदा हुई है)

3. We are going to Goa in summer holiday.

(हम गर्मियों की छुट्टियों में गोआ जा रहे हैं)

## 3. To – को

**(a) Use – किसी जगह को**

1. I am going to school.

(मैं स्कूल जा रहा हूँ)

2. Raman is going to the park.

(रमन पार्क जा रहा है)

## 4. On – ऊपर

**(a) Use – एक छोटी चीज़ का बड़ी चीज़ पर रखा होना**

1. Flower vase is kept on the table.

(फूलों का गुलदान मेज़ पर रखा है)

2. Mobile is lying on the bed.

(मोबाइल बैड पर पड़ा है)

**(b) Day and date के साथ**

1. I went on Tuesday.

   (मैं मंगलवार को गया था)

2. He was born on 20th may 2007.

   (वह 20 मई 2001 को पैदा हुआ था)

**Note**- Date के साथ 'on' लगता है, पर साल के साथ 'in' लगता है। जब date और साल इक्टठे दिया हो तो 'on' लगता है क्योंकि date पहले आती है।

**(c) किसी तरफ**

1. I was standing on the pavement.

   (मैं फुटपाथ पर खड़ा था)

2. She was standing on the left.

   (वह बाँयी ओर खड़ी थी)

**5. At**

**(a) Use- समय के साथ (निश्चित)**

With pair of time.

1. I was born at 7 pm.

   (मैं 7 बजे पैदा हुआ था)

2. Tiara will come home at 10 pm.

   (टियारा दस बजे घर आएगी)

**(b) छोटी जगह के साथ**

(With small places)

1. He has gone to pick his uncle at railway station.

   (वह अपने अंकल को लेने रेलवे स्टेशन गया है)

2. She works at a hotel.

(वह होटल में काम करती है)

Note:- " In" बड़ी जगह के साथ होता है जैसे कोई शहर या देश। छोटी जगह के साथ 'at' use होता है।

**(c) रात और दोपहर के साथ**

(With night and noon)

1. I like to study at night.

(मुझे रात को पड़ना अच्छा लगता है)

2. Parineeta was here at noon.

(परिनिता दोपहर को यहाँ थी)

**(d) मूल्य के लिए**

(To tell cost of something)

1. This banana is sold at 30rs per kg.

(यह केला 30 रुपये दर्जन के हिसाब से मिल रहे हैं)

**(e) किसी त्योहार या खास अवसर पर**

(In any festival / event)

1. I will come home at Diwali.

(मैं दिवाली पर घर जाऊँगी)

2. He is invited at his birthday.

(वह उसके जन्मदिन पर आंमत्रित है)

6. **Under नीचे**

(a) किसी के नीचे पर बिना पूरी तरह हुए

(Under something, but not touched)

1. Shyam is sitting under the tree.
   (शाम पेड़ के नीचे बैठा है)
2. Tinku is hiding under the bed.
   (टिंकू पलंग के नीचे छूपा है)

**7. Between**

Use- **दो के बीच में**

(Between two people or objects)

1. Kiara is sitting between Kapil and Seema.
   (कियारा कपिल और सीमा के बीच में बैठीं  है)
2. Please distribute this between you both.
   (ये चीज़ दोनों में बाँट लो)

**8. <u>Among (बीच में)</u>**

Use- दो से अधिक के बीच में

(More than two people or objects)

1. The Sweet were distributed among the class.
   (मिठाई सारी क्लास में बाँट दी गयी)
2. This book is kept on shelf among other books.
   (उसकी किताब रैक पर किताबों में पड़ी है)

**9. <u>With (से) (के साथ)</u>**

**(a) Usage – से**

1. I cut the apple with a knife.
   (मैंने चाकू से सेब काटा)

2. Shree wrote the poem with red pen.

(श्री ने कविता लाल पैन से लिखी थी)

**(b)** Accompanying- **किसी के साथ**

1. My brother went to office with his colleague.

(मेरा भाई अपने सहकर्मो के साथ आफिस गया)

2. I am with you in this matter.

(मैं इस मुद्दे में  तुम्हारे साथ हूँ)

3. Prerna is going to the fest with Meera.

(प्रेरणा मेले में मीरा के साथ जा रही है)

**10.** For

**(a)** Use - **समय की अवधि**

Duration of time

1. He is trying for job.

(वह नौकरी के लिए कोशिश कर रहा है)

2. Geeta has been studying for 3 hours.

(गीता 3 घंटे से पढ़ रही है)

**(b) के लिए** (for any purpose)

1. He is asking me for money.

(वह मुझसे पैसे के लिए पूछ रहा है)

2. I bought a cake for you.

(मैं तुम्हारे लिए केक लाया हूँ)

**(c) किसी चीज़ के बदले में**

(In exchange)

1. She bought this dress for Rs 500.

   (वह ये पोशाक 500 रूपये की लायी है)

2. I gave 10,000 for this mobile.

   (मैंने 10,000 रूपये दिए मोबाईल के लिए)

**11.** By

(a) use- द्वारा

(By someone)

1. This decoration is done by him.

   (यह सजावट उसने की है)

2. This book is gifted by my father.

   (यह किताब मेरे पापा ने मुझे भेंट की है)

**(b) से** go, travel

1. I travelled by bus.

   (मैंने बस से यात्रा की)

2. Sheetal came here by taxi.

   (शीतल टैक्सी से यहाँ आयी थी)

**(c) तक**

1. I finished this project by noon.

   (मैंने दोपहर तक यह प्रोजेक्ट खत्म किया)

2. Ram will leave by 3o' clock.

   (राम 3 बजे तक निकल जाएगा)

**12. <u>Since से</u>**

Since का प्रयोग निश्चित समय के साथ होता है, पर वो अब तक चलना चाहिए जैसे रहा, रही रहे हैं।

Since is used for specific time but it should be continuous.

1. He has been trying for job since long.
   (वह काम के लिए काफी देर से तलाश कर रहा है)
2. I have been working in this company since 2014.
   (मैं इस कम्पनी में 2014 से काम कर रहा हूँ)

**13. <u>Before- पहले</u>**

**(a) use – पहले**

1. She went before the party started.
   (वह पार्टी शुरू होने से पहले चली गयी)
2. This train will reach before time.
   (यह ट्रेन समय से पहले पहुँचेगी)

**(b) सामने होना-(In front of)**

1. His enemy stood before him.
   (उसका दुश्मन उसके सामने खड़ा था)
2. She was sitting before me.
   (वह मेरे सामने बैठी थी)

**14. <u>After- बाद में</u>**

(a) Use- बाद में

1. I will reach just after you.
   (मैं तुम्हारे बाद पहुँच जाऊँगा)

2. I will reach office after 9 am today.

(आज मैं आफिस 9 बजे के बाद पहुँचूँगा)

**(b)** Use - **किसी के पीछे पड़ जाना**

(To be after someone)

1. He was after that girl.

(वह उस लड़की के पीछे पड़ा हुआ था)

2. I am after my father to buy me a watch.

(मैंने अपने पापा के पीछे पड़ा हूँ घड़ी खरीदने के लिए)

# Worksheet Prepositions

Fill in the blanks using prepositions from the word bank

| From | to | buy | with | in | On |
|---|---|---|---|---|---|
| for | of | since | before | after | |

1. I have been studying in this school ............. 2015.
2. I like to spend time ............. my dog.
3. He gave me a pen ............. my birthday.
4. I went ............. the doctor yesterday.
5. Neeraj went ............. Goa ............. summer holidays.
6. I went ............. market ............. my family.
7. I got a watch ............. my sister.
8. This drawing is done ............. me.
9. He is playing football ............. 2015.
10. Her birthday is ............. 11th june.
11. The train will reach ............. time.
12. I will come ............. you.

# Three form of verbs (क्रिया के रूप)

**Verb** - a verb is a kind of word that tells about an action or state.

**क्रिया** - इस शब्द अथवा शब्द समूह के द्वारा किसी कार्य के होने अथवा किया जाने का बोध हो।

Three form of verbs

| First Form | Second Form | Third Form | In Hindi |
|---|---|---|---|
| Visit | Visited | Visited | देखने जाना |
| Eat | Ate | Eaten | खाना |
| See | Saw | Seen | देखना |
| Work | Worked | Worked | कार्य करना |
| Wash | Washed | Washed | धोना |
| Feel | Felt | Felt | महसूस करना |
| Watch | Watched | Watched | निगरानी रखना या देखना |
| keep | kept | Kept | रखना |
| Come | Came | Come | आना |
| Go | Went | Gone | जाना |
| Know | Knew | Known | जानना |
| Sell | Sold | Sold | बेचना |
| Fly | Flew | Flown | उड़ना |
| Stand | Stood | Stood | खड़े होना |

| Tell | Told | Told | बताना |
|---|---|---|---|
| Teach | Taught | Taught | पड़ना |
| Tell | Told | Told | बताना |
| Hear | Heard | Heard | सुनना |
| Grow | Grew | Grown | बड़ना |
| Forget | Forgot | Forgotten | भूलना |
| Leave | Left | Left | छोड़ना |
| Sleep | Slept | Slept | सोना |
| Sit | Sat | Sat | बैठना |
| Speak | Spoke | Spoken | बोलना |
| Take | Took | Taken | लेकर जाना |
| Lose | Lost | Lost | खो जाना |
| Swim | Swam | Swum | तैरना |
| Fight | Fought | Fought | लड़ना |
| Beat | Beat | Beaten | मारना |
| Ride | rode | Ridden | चलना |
| Say | Said | Said | बोलना |
| rise | Rose | Risen | उठना |
| Break | Broke | Broken | तोड़ना |
| Blow | Blew | Blown | हवा का बहना,<br>फट जाना |
| Bite | Bit | Bitten | काटना |
| Awake | Awoke | Awoken | जागना |
| Arrive | Arrived | Arrived | पहुँचना |

| Abuse | Abused | Abused | गाली देना |
|---|---|---|---|
| Allow | Allowed | Allowed | आज्ञा देना |
| Appear | Appeared | Appeared | प्रकट होना |
| Begin | Began | Begun | शुरू करना |
| Throw | Threw | Thrown | फैंकना |
| Run | Ran | Run | भागना |
| Wear | Wore | Worn | पहनना |
| Write | Wrote | Written | लिखना |
| Drive | Drove | Driven | चलाना |
| Lay | Laid | Laid | देना |
| Lie | Lied | Lied | झूठ बोलना |
| Call | Called | Called | बुलाना, फोन करना |
| Cut | Cut | Cut | काटना |
| Put | Put | Put | डालना |
| Read | Read | Read | पढ़ना |
| Boil | Boiled | Boiled | उबालना |
| Believe | Believed | Believed | मानना |
| Dance | Danced | Danced | नापना |
| Clear | Cleared | Cleared | साफ करना |
| Celebrate | Celebrated | Celebrated | मनाना |
| Like | Liked | Liked | पसन्द करना |

# Tenses

Tenses are of three forms

Tenses तीन प्रकार के होते हैं।

1. <u>Present tense (वर्तमान काल)</u>
2. <u>Past tense (भूत काल)</u>
3. <u>Future tense (भविष्य काल)</u>

## Present tense

Present tense is of four types.

Present tense के चार प्रकार के होते हैं।

1. **Present indefinite tense/ simple present tense**

   Simple present tense is used to tell about any activity /work which happens regularly.

   Simple present tense का प्रयोग आदत, नियमित या स्वभाविक कार्य को बताने के लिए किया जाता है।

   Rule- first form of verb + (S) in case of one person.

### For example / जैसे कि

1. मोहन स्कूल जाता है।

   Mohan goes to school.

2. वह सारा दिन मूवी देखता है।

   He watches movie the whole day.

3. वे पार्क में खेलते हैं।

   They play in the park.

## (A) Negative simple present tense sentences

जहाँ नहीं का प्रयोग होता है वह negative sentence है।

Rule- do/does + not + verb first form

For one person

For example / जैसे कि

1. वह सुबह नहीं उठता है।

   He does not get up in the morning.

2. तुम मुझे फोन नहीं करते हो।

   You do not call me.

**Note-** you / I are one but we do not use "does" with them.

3. मैं अब फुटबॉल खेलने नहीं जाता हुँ।

   I do not go to play football.

## (B) Interrogative simple present tense

जहां कोई सवाल पूछा जाता है उसे interrogative sentence बोलते हैं। जब present / वर्तमान के लिए सवाल पूछा जाता है तो उसमें interrogative simple present tense का प्रयोग होता है।

When question is asked that's called a interrogative sentence when question is asked for present then we use interrogative simple present tense.

**Rule –** sentence Begin with do / does + not + verb first form.

वाक्य की शुरुआत do / does से + not + verb की पहली form

For example / जैसे कि

1. क्या रेखा स्कूल जाती है?

   Does Rekha go to school?

2. क्या तुम उसे नहीं बुलाते हो?

   Do you not call him now?

3. क्या वह रोज पड़ता है?

   Does he study daily?

(C)W.H type question - **प्रश्नवाचक शब्द**

Was, what, where, why, when, how वाले question

Rule- w. H word +do/ does +verb first form

1. तुम क्या करते हो?

   What do you do?

2. प्रिया ऑफिस क्यों नहीं आती?

   Why does Priya not come to the office?

3. उन्होंने यह कैसे किया?

   How do they do this work?

2. Present continuous tense

Present continuous tense is used when we are talking about the present which is still continuing.

Present continuous tense का प्रयोग ऐसे कार्यों के लिए होता है जो अभी भी चल रहे हो।

**Rule** - is/am/are +(verb first form+ ing)

1. मैं कहानी लिख रहा हूँ।

   I am writing a story.

2. राधा पढ़ रही है।

   Radha is studying.

3. वे मैदान में खेल रहे हैं।

   They are playing in the ground.

(A) <u>Interrogative present continuous</u>

**Rule-** (is / am / are + (verb firs form + ing)

1. क्या तुम कल दिल्ली जा रहे हो?

   Are you going to Delhi tomorrow?

2. क्या वह खाना बना रहा है?

   Is he cooking food?

3. क्या ये आज स्कूल आ रहे हैं?

   Are they coming to school today?

(B) <u>W.H. Word type question present continuous</u>

**Rule-** (is / am / are + (verb first form + ing)

1. क्या तुम आज घर वापिस नहीं आ रहे हो?

   Are you not coming back home today?

2. तुम कहाँ जा रहे हो?

   Where are you today?

3. वह फोन पर किससे बात कर रहा है?

   Whom is he talking on phone?

4. तुम्हारा भाई आजकल कहाँ रह रहा है?

   Where is your brother living nowadays?

3. <u>Present Perfect tense</u>

Present Perfect tense is used which is finished within short interval and is used in present.

Present perfect tense का प्रयोग ऐसे कार्यों के लिए किया जाता रहे जो तुरंत खत्म हुआ हो और वर्तमान में हो जैसे कि है क्या प्रयोग हो।

**Rule** - subject + has/ have /+ verb third form

<u>For example / **जैसे कि**</u>

1. वह ऑफिस आ चुका है

   He has come to the office.

2. मैं इस होटल में आ चुका हुँ।

   I have come to this hotel or I have visited this hotel.

3. उसने मेरी मदद की है।

   He has helped me.

4. वह सब वापिस घर जा चुके हैं।

   They all have gone to their house.

(A) <u>Interrogative present perfect tense</u>

**(Yes/ no sentences)**

Rule- has/have + subject + (not) if required + third form of verb.

<u>For example / **जैसे कि**</u>

1. क्या वह नौकरी छोड़ चुका है?

   Has he left the job?

2. क्या तुम उसको लेने नहीं गये?

   Have you not gone to pick her?

3. क्या माँ ने खाना खा लिया?

   Has mom eaten the food?

(B) W. H word type questions (Present Perfect)

**Rule** - W. H word+ has/ have + subject +(not) + verb third form

1. वह कौन से कॉलेज में जा रहा है?

   Which college has he gone to?

2. यह ड्रेस कौन सी दुकान में खरीदा?

   Where have you bought this dress from?

3. तुम वहाँ कैसे आए?

   How have you come?

4. Present Perfect Continuous tense

This tense is used when some work / activity is continuing from the past and is still continuing in the present.

Present perfect continuous tense का प्रयोग किसी ऐसे कार्य के लिए किया जाता है जो पहले भूतकाल में शुरू हुआ हो ओर अब तक यदि वर्तमान तक जारी रहे।

**Rule**- (subject + has/have +(not) + been + (verb first form + ing)

For example / जैसे कि

1. मैं जिम में जाता जा रहा हूँ।

   I have been going to the gym.

2. राजन दो घंटे से नाश्ता बना रहा है।

   Rajan has been cooking food for two hours.

3. मैं सुबह से तुम्हारा इंतजार कर रही हूँ।

   I have been waiting for you since morning.

(C) <u>Interrogative sentences present perfect continuous</u>

**Rule** - (has / have + subject + (not) been + (verb first form +ing)

1. क्या तुम सुबह से किसी का इंतजार कर रहे हो?

   Have you been waiting for someone since morning?

2. क्या वह कल से पड़ाई कर रहा है?

   Has he been studying since yesterday?

3. क्या वे एक दूसरे से दो दिन से बात नहीं कर रहे हैं?

   Have they not been talking to each other for two days?

## Present Perfect Continuous tense

**Present Perfect Continuous tense** का प्रयोग किसी ऐसे कार्य के लिए किया जाता है, जो पहले भूतकाल में शुरू हुआ हो और अब तक यानि वर्तमान तक जारी रहे।

**Rule** - [subject +has / have + (not) + been + (verb first form+ing)

For Example - जैसे कि

1. मैं जिम में जाती जा रही हूँ – I have been going to the gym.
2. राजन दो घंटे से नाश्ता बना रहा है - Rajan has been cooking food for two hours.
3. मै सुबह से तुम्हारा इन्तज़ार कर रही हूं - I have been waiting for you since morning.

a) Interrogative sentence Present Perfect Continuous

**Rule - (Has / Have + Subject + (not) been (verb first form+ing)**

For Example - जैसे कि

1. क्या तुम सुबह से किसी का इंतजार कर रहे हो?

   Have you been waiting for someone since morning?
2. क्या वह कल से पड़ाई कर रहा है?

   Has he been studying since yesterday?
3. क्या वे एक दूसरे से दो दिन से बात नहीं कर रहे हैं?

   Have they not been talking to each other since two days?

b) W.H. Word type questions present perfect continuous

**Rule** - W.H. word & has / have + subject + (not) + been + (verb first form + ing)

For Example - **जैसे कि**

1. वह पिछले दस साल से कहाँ है?

   Where have he been for last ten years?

2. तुम कब से शादीशुदा हो?

   How long have you been married?

3. पिछले पाँच साल से वे क्या कर रहे है?

   What have they been doing for the last five years?

## PAST TENSE

### Past Indefinite or simple Past tense

Simple Part tense is used when we talk about something which used to happen regularly but not any more.

Simple Past tense हम तब प्रयोग करते हैं, जब कोई काम के बारे में बताया जाए जो पहले होता रहता था पर अब नहीं होता।

**Rule -** Subject + verb second form

**Note-** with one person or more the second form of verb does not change. It remains the same.

एक व्यक्ति या अधिक व्यक्ति के साथ verb का दूसरा रूप बदलता नहीं। दोनों के साथ वही प्रयोग किया जाता हैं ।

For Example - **जैसे कि**

1. वह स्कूल गया था।

   He went to school.

2. सीता रोज मंदिर जाती थी।

   Sita went to temple daily.

3. मैं कल डॉक्टर के पास गयी थी।

I went to the doctor yesterday.

a) Interrogative sentence Simple Past Tense

**Rule- Did + Subject + (not) + verb first form.**

In Questions since the third form of "do" is already used, so we use verb first form.

सवालों में क्योंकि "do" की third form यानि "did" लग जाती है तो इसलिए Verb की first form (पहला रूप) ही लगता है।

For Example - **जैसे कि**

1. क्या तुम वहाँ नहीं गये?

   Did you not go there?
2. क्या तुम मेरे लिए पोशाक लेकर आए?

   Did you get the dress for me?
3. क्या वह ऑफिस नहीं आया था?

   Did he not come to office?

b) W.H. Word type questions Simple past tense

**Rule – W.H. word + was/were +subject + (not) + verb first form**

For Example - **जैसे कि**

1. उसने कल क्या किया?

   What did he do yesterday?

2. कल गीता ने कितना काम खत्म किया?

   How much work did Geeta finish yesterday?

3. कौन सी किताब उन्होंने नहीं पढ़ी थी?

   Which book did they not read?

2. <u>Past Continuous tense</u>

   Past Continues tense is used for any work or activity which was happening continuously but not anymore.

   Past continuous tense उस कार्य के लिए प्रयोग होता है जो हो रहा था पर अब नहीं।

   **Rule - subject + was / were + (verb first form + ing)**

   Was- For one person or thing

   Were - For more than one /you/I

<u>For Example - **जैसे कि**</u>

1. वह मूवी देख रही थी।

   She was watching a movie.

2. मोहन रो रहा था।

   Mohan was crying.

3. वे मार्केट जा रहे थे।

   They were going to the market.

a) <u>Interrogative sentences- Past Continuous tense</u>

   **Rule** - Subject I was / were + Subject + (not) + 'Verb first form + ing

For Example - जैसे कि

1. क्या तुम खाना नहीं बना रही थी?

   Were you not cooking the food?

2. क्या तुम इस स्कूल में काउंसलर थी?

   Were you working as a counselor in that school?

3. क्या वह रात भर काम कर रहा था?

   Was he working the whole night yesterday?

b) W.H. word type Question

Rule - W.H. word (like why / how/when/what) + was/ were + subject +(verb first form + ing)

1. तुम कल सारा दिन क्या कर रही थी ?

   What were you doing the whole day yesterday?

2. वह क्या खा रहा था?

   What was he eating?

3. वे कल किन लोगों से बात कर रहे थे?

   Whom were they talking to yesterday?

3. Past Perfect Tense

Past perfect tense is used for any work or activity which had finished a long time ago.

Present past perfect tense का प्रयोग ऐसे कार्यों के लिए किया जाता है जो काफी देर से खत्म हो चुके थे।

Rule - Subject + had + (not) + verb third form.

For Example - जैसे कि

1. वह यह शहर काफी देर से छोड़ चुका था

   He had left this city since long time.

2. मेरे स्टेशन पहुँचने से पहले गाड़ी छूट चुकी थी

   The train had left before I reached the station.

3. मैं यह समाचार पहले ही सुन चुका था

   I had already heard this news.

a) Interrogative Sentence - Past Perfect tense

Rule – Had/ Subject (not) + verb third form

1. क्या वह यह जगह छोड़ चुका था?

   Had he left this place?

2. क्या तुम स्कूल जा चुके थे?

   Had you gone to school?

3. क्या गीता गाना गा चुकी थी?

   Had Geeta sung the song?

b) W.H word type Questions

Rule – W.H. Word + Subject + (not) + Verb third form

1. पंकज पहले से कौन सी खबर सुन चुका था

   Which news had Pankaj heard already?

2. तुम्हारे किस पाठ पढ़ने से पहले अध्यापक ने क्या कहा

   What had teacher said before you read the chapter.

3. हमारे आने के बाद ड्राइवर कार कहाँ ले गया था

   Where did the driver go after we had arrived back?

4. उसके गाँव जाने के बाद तुमसे मिलने कौन आया?

   Who came to meet you after he had gone to village?

## 4. Past Perfect Continuous tense

Past Perfect Continuous tense shows that an action that started in the past Continued up until another time in the past.

Past Perfect Continuous tense से हमें ज्ञात होता है कि कोई कार्य भूतकाल
में शुरू हुआ था और जारी था अर्थात कार्य पूर्ण था। इस Tense में समय का वर्णन भी होता है ।

**Rule – Subject + Had been + (Verb +ing) first form.**

1. वह सुबह दो घंटे से पढ़ रहा था।

   He had been studying since morning.

2. हम 2 घंटे से इंतजार कर रही थी।

   I had been waiting for two hours.

3. हम 1 घंटे से कपड़े धो रहे थे।

   We had been washing the clothes for an hour.

### a) Interrogative sentences - Past Perfect Continuous.

Rule - Had + subject + been + (verb first form+ing)

1. क्या वह दो घंटे से सो रहा था?

   Had he been sleeping for 2 hours?

2. क्या शाम से बारिश हो रही थी?

   Had it been raining since evening?

3. क्या वे 5 घंटे से क्रिकेट खेल रहे थे?

   Had they been playing cricket for five hours?

**b)** <u>W.H. word type Questions - Past Perfect continuous</u>

**Rule** – W.H word + had + Subject + been + (verb + ing) + object + other word + since + for time.

<u>For Example - **जैसे कि**</u>

1. पापा जी शाम से क्या कर रहे थे?

   What had Papa been doing since evening?

2. अरुनिमा तीन घंटे से कौन सा उपन्यास पढ़ रही थी?

   Which novel had Arunima been reading for the past three hours?

3. बच्चे रविवार को कौन सी मूवी देख रहे थे?

   Which movie had children been watching on Sunday?

## FUTURE TENSE

1. <u>Future Indefinite / simple future Tense –</u>

   Future Indefinite or simple future tense is used to describe work/ activity which is going to happen in future.

   Future tense का प्रयोग हम भविष्य में होने वाले कार्य के लिए करते हैं।

   **Rule - subject + will + (not) + verb first form**

For Example - **जैसे कि**

1. मैं कल स्कूल नहीं जाऊँगा।

   I will not go to school tomorrow.

2. अब वह अच्छी अंग्रेजी बोलेगा।

   He will speak good English now.

3. वह कल यहाँ आएगा।

   He will come here tomorrow.

**a)** Interrogative sentences - simple future Tense

Rule - will + subject + (not) + verb first form.

1. क्या तुम यहाँ जॉब करोगे?

   Will you do a job here?

2. क्या तुम्हारी बहन इस कॉलेज में पढ़ेगी?

   Will your sister study in this college?

3. क्या वह कल पार्टी में आऐगें?

   Will they come to the party tomorrow?

**b)** WH Word type Questions - future (simple) Tense

Rule – W.H. word + object + will + subject + verb first form

For Example - **जैसे कि**

1. वे कब आएँगे ?

   When will they come?

2. वे कौन सा गाना गाएंगे

   Which Song will they sing?

3. तुम अब नीता को कहाँ ढूँढ़ोगे

Where will you find out Neeta?

2. Future Continuous Tense

Rule – Subject + will be + (Verb first form + ing)

For Example - **जैसे कि**

1. वह क्रिकेट खेल रहा होगा

   He will be playing cricket.

2. वह दिल्ली जा रहा होगी

   She will be going to Delhi.

3. वे भारत छोड़कर जा रहे होंगे

   They will be leaving India.

**a)** Interrogative tense - Future Continuous Tense

Rule - will + subject + be (verb+ ing)

For Example - **जैसे कि**

1. क्या वह काम कर रहा होगा?

   Will he be doing the work?

2. क्या उसे पता चल गया होगा?

   Will he be knowing about it?

3. क्या तुम उसे लेने जाओगे?

   Will you be going to pick him up?

**b)** W. H. word type Questions - future continues tense

Rule - W.H. word + will + subject + be + (verb +ing)

1. तुम वहाँ क्यों नहीं जा रहे होगे?

   Why will you not be going there?

2. वे क्या काम कर रहे होंगे?

   What work will they be doing?

3. वे दिल्ली कैसे जा रहे होंगे?

   How will they be going to Delhi?

3. Future Perfect Tease.

   Rule - Subject + will have + verb third form

For Example - **जैसे कि**

1. पिताजी आफिस से आ गये होंगें।

   Father will have come from office.

2. तुमने उसे इस प्रपोजल के बारे में बताया होगा।

   You will have told him about this proposal.

3. मै यह किताब खत्म कर चुकी होगी।

   I will have finished this book.

**a)** Interrogative sentences - Future Perfect tense.

Rule - Will + subject + have + & verb third form.

For Example - **जैसे कि**

1. क्या वह यह काम कर चुका होगा?

   Will he have done this work?

2. क्या वह घर आ गया होगा?

   Will he have come home?

3. क्या उसे यह पाठ याद हो चुका होगा?

   Will she have learnt this chapter?

**b)** <u>W.H. Type questions - Future Perfect Tense.</u>

Rule – W.H. question word + will + subject + have + verb third form

1. वह कहाँ चला गया होगा?

   Where will he have gone?

2. वह क्या खा चुकी होगी?

   What will she have eaten?

3. तुम कहाँ पहुँच चुके होगे?

   Where will you have reached?

4. <u>Future Perfect Continuous tense</u>

Rule - subject + will + have been + (verb first form + ing)

<u>For Example - **जैसे कि**</u>

1. वह दो घण्टे से तुम्हारा इंतजार कर रही होगी।

   She will have been waiting for you for two hours.

2. वह सुबह से ऑफिस में काम रही होगी।

   She will have been working in the office since morning.

3. वह चार साल से इस शहर में रह रहा होगा।

   He will have been living in this city for four years.

2. <u>Interrogative sentences - Future Perfect continuous tense</u>

Rule- will + subject + have been + (Verb +ing)

<u>For Example - जैसे कि</u>

1. क्या वह इस तरह काम कर रहा होगा?

   Will he have been working like this?

2. क्या वह अब तक लिखती रही रोगी?

   Will she have been writing till now?

3. क्या वह मुझे याद कर रहा होगा?

   Will he have been remembering me?

a) <u>W.H. type questions. Future Perfect continuous tense</u>

Rule – W.H word + will + Subject + (not) + have been + (verb + ing)

<u>For Example - जैसे कि</u>

1. वह दो दिन से घर क्यों नहीं आ रहा होगा।

   Why will he not have been coming to his house?

2. वह क्यों नहीं पढ़ रही होगी।

   Why will she not have been studying?

3. वे मुंबई क्यों नही जा रहे होंगें?

   Why will they not have been going to Mumbai?

# PART B

## INTRODUCTION TO STORY WRITING (FROM HINDI TO ENGLISH)

# Story writing
# कहानी लेखन

कहानी लेखन वह रूप है लिखने का जो की बहुत रोचक है और जिसके द्वारा हमें कहानी पता चलती है। क्योंकि कहानी हम पिछली बातों की बताते हैं तो इसमें Past tense का प्रयोग होता है। Simple Past tense जिसमें "था" वाले वाक्य हो । "चुके थे " जब वाक्य के अंत में आता है तो Past Perfect का प्रयोग होता है। कभी कभी कहानी में बताया जाता है कि कोई कुछ कर रहा था तभी वह आ गया था ऐसे वाक्य में शुरूआत में Past Continuous क्योंकि "रहा था" आता है और फिर आखिरी भाग में Past Perfect या support simple Past tense का प्रयोग होता है

Story- writing is a very interesting form of writing through which we get to know about stories of the past. As stories mostly represent the incidents occurred in the past, that is why mostly "Past tense" is used. When something happened or done then simple Past tense is used and where things were already over then "Past Perfect" is used. If someone is doing something, when something else had already happened then we tend to use present Continuous tense just followed by past perfect tense. Things will become clearer when we will practice story writing.

# The Elephants & the Ants
# हाथी और चीटियाँ

Try to do this all by yourself first.

एक बार बहुत घमण्डी हाथी सब छोटे जानवरों को धमकाता था। वह अपने घर के नज़दीक चीटियों की पहाड़ी पर जाकर सब चीटियों पे अपनी सूँड से पानी डाल देता। चीटियाँ कुछ भी नहीं कर पाती बल्कि रोती रहती। हाथी हँसता और उनको धमकी देता कि वह उन्हें कुचल देगा। एक दिन चीटियों की बस हो गयी और उन्होंने हाथी को सबक सिखाने की ठानी। वह धीरे-धीरे उसकी सूँड में चली गयी और उसको काटने लगी। हाथी दर्द में गर्राया। उसको अपनी गलती का एहसास हो गया और उसने सब जानवरों से माफी माँगी ।

Once there lived an arrogant elephant who always bullied smaller animals. He used to go to ants hill near his home & spray water at the ants. The ants could not do anything but cried. The elephant laughed and threatened the ants that he would crush them to death. One day, the ants had enough and decided to teach the elephant a lesson. They slowly went into the elephant's trunk and started biting him.

The elephant howled in pain. He realized his mistake and apologized to ants and all the animal he had bullied.

# Slow & steady wins the race
# कछुआ और खरगोश

एक बार की बात है एक कछुआ था। वह बहुत धीरे-धीरे जंगल की तरफ जा रहा था जब खरगोश आया । खरगोश ने कछुए को रोककर उसकी धीमी चाल का बहुत मज़ाक उड़ाया। कछुए को बहुत बुरा लगा और उसने खरगोश का इस रेस करने की प्रतियोगिता स्वीकार कर ली । जब प्रतियोगिता शुरू हुई तो खरगोश छलांग मारकर दूर चला गया। कुछ देर बाद उसने पीछे देखा और पाया कि कछुआ नहीं दिख रहा था। वह थक गया और उसने एक पेड़ के नीचे सोने का निर्णय लिया। जब वह सो रहा था कछुए ने उसे देखा और धीरे-धीरे बढ़ता गया। जब खरगोश की नींद खुली तब तक कछुआ जीत चुका था।

Once upon a time, there was a tortoise. He was walking slowly back to the forest when a rabbit came. The rabbit stopped and laughed at the tortoise, making fun of his slow pace/walk. The tortoise felt bad and accepted the challenge of the race.

The race started. Rabbit hopped and after sometime he looked back and could not see the tortoise. He was tired and decided to sleep under the shade of a tree. By the time he was sleeping, the tortoise came slowly and left the rabbit behind. The rabbit woke up to find that the tortoise had won the race.

## Story from Hindi to English

# Where there is a will, there is a way /जहाँ चाह वहाँ राह

1. एक बार की बात है एक जंगल में एक कौआ रहता था।
2. वह बहुत प्यासा था।
3. उसने सारे जंगल में उड़कर पानी ढूँढा।
4. तब उसे एक सुराही घास पर पड़ी दिखी।
5. उसने अपनी चोंच सुराही में डाली पर पानी कम होने के कारण वह पानी तक नही पहुँच सका।
6. कौआ बहुत होशियार था।
7. उसने वहाँ पड़े कंकरों को सुराही में डाला।
8. इससे पानी ऊपर आ गया।
9. कौओ ने अपनी प्यास भुझायी और उड़ गया।

1. एक बार की बात है एक जंगल में एक कौआ रहता था

   (Sentence- Past Simple Tense)- Once upon a time there lived a crow in a jungle (second form of verb),
2. वह बहुत प्यासा था – (Simple Past tense.) He was very thirsty
3. उसने सारे जंगल में उड़कर पानी ढूँढा – (simple Past)– He flew over the whole jungle to find water.
4. तब उसे एक सुरोरी घास पर पड़ी दिखी- (simple past) – Then he found a vessel kept over the grass.
5. उसने अपनी चोंच सुराही में डाली पर पानी कम होने के कारण वह पानी तक नहीं पहुँच सका- He put his beak into the Vessel, but the

level of water in vessel was very low. Due to which he couldn't reach the water.

6. कौआ बहुत होशियार था Crow was very smart.
7. उसने वहाँ पड़े कंकरो को सुराही में डाला- He put the pebbles kept on ground into the vessel.
8. उससे पानी ऊपर आ गया - Due to which the water level rose/came up.
9. कौए ने, अपनी प्यास भुझायी और उड़ गया - Crow quenched his thirst and flew away.

## The cap seller & monkeys/ टोपी वाला और बंदर

एक बार एक टोपियाँ बेचने वाला था एक शहर में। टोपियाँ बेचने के बाद वह थक गया और घने वृक्ष की छाँव में सो गया। उस पेड़ पर बहुत सारे बंदर रहते थे और वह नीचे आया और टोपी वाले की सारी टोपियाँ उठाकर पहन ली जब टोपी वाला उठा तो उसने देखा कि टोकरी खाली थी। उसने ऊपर देखा तो सारे बंदर उसकी टोपी पहने थे। उसको सुझा कि बंदर नकल करते हैं। तो उसने अपनी टोपी नीचे फैक दी। उसको देखकर बंदरों ने भी अपनी टोपी नीचे फैक दी । टोपी वाले ने जल्दी से टोपी उठायी और टोकरी में डाली और घर खुशी-खुशी चला गया ।

Once upon a time there was a cap seller in a town. One day after selling the caps he got tired and slept under the shade of a big tree. There lived a lot of monkeys on that tree- They Came down and took all caps of Cap seller and wore them. When cap seller woke up, he saw that his basket was empty. He looked up and saw that all monkeys were wearing his cap. He realized that monkeys imitate a lot and repeat what the other person does. So he threw the Cap down. And Monkeys too threw their Caps down. The cap seller collected all the caps quickly and put them in the basket and went home happily.

# The Farmer who bought a well
# एक किसान जिसने कुंआ खरीदा

एक बार एक गरीब किसान ने एक अमीर आदमी से कुँआ खरीदा ताकि वह अपनी ज़मीन को पानी दे पाये। किसान ने जो भी कीमत अमीर आदमी ने माँगी, वह दे दी। अगले दिन जब किसान पानी कुँए से निकालने लगा तो अमीर आदमी ने उसे रोका और कहा कि तुमने कुँआ खरीदा है, कुँए का पानी नहीं। तो इस लिए तुम कुएँ का पानी नहीं निकाल सकते।

किसान को कुछ समझ में नहीं आया कि वह क्या करे तो वह राजा अकबर के दरबार पहुँचा और अकबर को अपनी दुविधा के बारे में बताया। अकबर ने बीरबल को यह केस सौंप दिया।

बीरबल उस अमीर आदमी के पास गया जिसने किसान को मुसीबत दी। अमीर आदमी ने जो किसान को कहा था वो भी बीरबल के सामने दोहरा दिया।

बीरबल ने जवाब दिया, "बहुत अच्छे जैसे कि तुमने किसान को कुँआ बेचा है तो तुम्हे या तो उसमें पानी रखने का किराया भरना पड़ेगा या वहाँ से पानी निकालकर कहीं और रखना पड़ेगा।

अमीर आदमी को पता चल गया कि बीरबल बहुत चालाक है और उसके सामने उसके चालाकी नहीं चलेगी तो उसने किसान को पानी इस्तेमाल करने की इजाजत दे दी।

## The farmer who bought a well/ एक किसान जिसने कुँआ खरीदा

A poor farmer once bought a well from a rich man, so that he could irrigate his land using the water from the well. The farmer paid the price quoted by the rich Man. The next day, When the farmer went to fetch water from the well, the rich man stopped him and disallowed him from drawing water. He said that the farmer had bought only the well and not water from him, so he cannot draw any water from the well.

Not knowing what to do, the farmer went to the king's court and told Akbar about it. Akbar handed over the case to Birbal.

Birbal then visited the rich man who was causing problems to the farmer. The rich Man repeated what he had told the farmer, to which Birbal said, "Very well, since you have sold the well and not water to the farmer, you will have to move all the water or "pay rent to the farmer to keep the water in the well""

The rich man realized that Birbal is very clever, and his shrewdness is not going to work. So he let the farmer use water from the well.

# PART C

## INTRODUCTION TO CREATIVE WRITING

# Introduction to creative writing/ सृजनात्मक-लेख

Creative writing is any writing which expresses your feelings, emotions and views. Mostly it is done through story telling or through poem. In this you can build characters through your imagination and create a story about them.

Types of Creative writing

- Poetry
- Plays
- Movies & television serial
- Short stories or Novels (Fiction)
- Personal essays.

There are techniques which can be used in creative will such as

- **Character development** – Imagining the characters and giving them different nature, looks, tracks & behaviour. Also how different changes over period of time. This requires lot of changes over period of time. This requires lot of observation & research. We can also model our characters based on real life people we know of.
- **Plot development** - The story as a whole and different parts should be planned. There should be a flow in the

story so that the reader can connect to it and it makes sense.

- **Vivid Setting** - When we tell a story then it should be able to convey the times or scene we are talking about. We should be able to make the reader imagine about the scene and characters, we can use five senses to convey. Sensory imagery explores the five human senses - Sound, taste, touch & smell. It includes the details of the scene to allow the reader to visualize and arrive at their own conclusion through imagery clues.

- **Different types of sensory imagery.**

1. <u>Visual imagery -</u> This includes explanation in detail about the physical features of a thing or human or place like colour, size, shape, shade, light men, darkness etc.

<u>Example:-</u>

- ❖ Bright red roses
- ❖ Lush green grass
- ❖ Tall dark gentleman
- ❖ Narrow Street
- ❖ Palatial house
- ❖ Tiny girl with a pony-tail.

2. Gustatory imagery - This defines tastes. This can include five basic tastes - sweet, salty, bitter and sour.

   Like - The sweet rasgulla melted in my mouth.

   The food tasted delicious.

3. Tactile imagery- This means what you can feel on skin. Feeling different sensation or different is temperature is part of tactile imagery.

For e.g - The hot sun piercing through my skin.

The Sun rays giving warmth on a winter day.

The Pillow feels cold against my flushed face.

4. Auditory imagery- It includes sense of hearing. The different sounds can define the scene very well.

For e.g - The sound of laughter.

The dog barking could be heard down the Street.

The screams got louder.

5. Olfactory imagery - This includes the smell. It helps to describe the place we are in.

   The fragrance of roses.

   Her perfumes smelled like Vanilla.

   The fragrance of soil coming after rain.

6. Underlying theme - The theme of story /poetry can be honesty, love, romantic, war, revenge or moral oriented. So before writing we should be clear about the theme.

## Let's re-write some Stories with creative writing
## The thirsty Crow

The crow flapped its black wings and soared the sky under the rays of glistening sun. But soon its playful flight turned into a search for water as he felt parched. It scanned the forest and finally its gaze landed on a tall vessel sitting on the lush green grass. It flapped its wings harder to rush to the vessel. However the tall neck of the vessel didn't allow its beak to reach water. The splashing sound of water inside the vessel as a result his struggle made him grow more thirsty. He knew in such circumstances calmnes is the key. So he calmed himself and ponder over. Suddenly he spotted pebbles which were scattered across the nearby road. One by one it dropped the pebbles into the vessel, splashing the water each time. Gradually the level of water increased and crow could quenth its thirst. The water felt refreshing and turned it playful again. The crow spread it dark wings again to touch the zenith of the sky.

Home work - Underline the tough words & find its meaning. Make a note of it in your notebook.

1. Try making a story with the help of these keywords.

| | |
|---|---|
| Roaring Cats & Dogs | Cleaning the mud |
| Puddles on the street | Pat it dry |
| tiny dog | Gave luke- warm |
| drenched | walk |
| Under Tree | Play together |
| Gopal Kind Nature | Naughty Pet |
| Picked the Dog | best friends forever |
| Gave it bath with warm water | |

2.

Lazy Uday

Uday - Define how he looks like?

- Define his nature by talking about some instances like he fails to reach school on time as could not get on time.
- Define what he is wearing by expressing the colour and all?

School - Say about how the school is -big/ small with grounds and garden?

Why Uday got punishment?

Class - How Uday didn't study?

Why he did not study?

What he realised during exams?

How did he do in exams?

3.

Write a Story about honesty.

- Create a character on which story is written.
- Mention Circumstances too
- How honesty is the best virtue?

4.

Write about your favourite moment or holiday or any favourite memory. Re-Create and use imagination and five senses imagery.

# PART D

## INTRODUCTION TO EMAIL WRITING AND INFORMAL MESSAGE WRITING

# E-Mail
# ईमेल

There are two types of mails

- Formal e-mail
- Informal e- Mail

Formal e-mail is an e -mail which is written to school authorities, companies, government department and offices.

Informal e-mail- are written to relatives and friends.

**Example of Formal e-mails**

Write an e-mail to your manager/ teacher asking for two days leave.

Dear Sir / Ma'am

This is to inform you that I am planning to take leave for two days i.e. on 27th Jan 2023 and 28th Jan 2023 on account of some personal work which needs my urgent attention.

I will be highly obliged if you can grant me leave for the mentioned dates. Hoping to hear from you soon.

Thanks & Regards

XYZ – (Name)

(Position in company or class you study in)

1. Write an e-mail for applying for the post in an organization.

Dear Sir / Ma'am

I am hereby applying for the post of Assistant Manager- Product marketing in your esteemed organisation as I have learnt about the vacancy as well as your requirement for the job from your online advertisement.

I would love to be associated with your esteemed organisation. I am hereby attaching my resume. Hoping to hear from you soon.

Thanks & Regards

XYZ – (Name)

(Mobile Number)

2. Write an e-mail for asking for the meeting.

Dear Sir / Ma'am

I represent XYZ bank. I am working as an Investment Manager. I would like to express my gratitude to you for banking with us and provide us with the opportunity of serving you.

There are many investment schemes provided by our bank which can enable you to have better earnings on your investment. I would like to have an appointment with you so that I can apprise you about these investment opportunities. Looking forward to serve you and hearing from you.

Thanks & Regards

XYZ – (Name)

(Position)

(Mobile Number)

3. Write an e-mail for complaining about the defective product.

Dear Sir/Ma'am

This is in regard to the shopping which I did recently on your website through online. I have always admired the quality of footwear of your company. But recently I have had the chance of having bad experience with the product as well as the service of your company. The pair of shoes I received was defective, so I called on the helpline number and complained about it. Despite complaining innumerable times, nothing has been done so far.

I am writing this to you after such a bitter experience. Please make sure my shoe is either returned or replaced or my money gets refunded. I am hereby attaching the order number, picture of shoes as well as the complaint number. Hopefully now things will move at fast pace. Kindly do the needful asap.

Regards

Name

Mobile no

# Informal messages/ अनौपचारिक संदेश

These days we use social media chat rooms to send informal messages to our family, friends, relatives, acquaintances and even to our suspects, colleagues & subordinates

<u>Let's first see how you guest</u>

1. Greeting (example)
   - Hi
   - Hello
   - Hey
   - Good Morning / Good Afternoon / Good evening

2. Message (example)
   - How you doing?
   - How are you?
   - How is everything at your end?
   - What's happening? (with friends you are in regular touch with)
   - Hope everything is fine with you. (in case you want to instruct/ Message)
   - What are you up to? (asking about plans) or ask something after this)

3. Sub-message.
    - It's been long (It means It's been long time since you both have talked to each other)
    - I was remembering you yesterday only or today only (When you want to tell the other person that you think about him/her)

While asking for some favour (examples)

1. I was wondering if you could lend me your book for a week?
2. Can I borrow your jacket (white) from you?
3. Do you mind if I borrow your juicer?
4. Could you lend me your car for today?

Asking Statement (examples)

1. Would you be coming to school today?
2. Can you pick me up from school today?
3. Shall I bring something to eat?
4. Do you want me to bring that book?
5. When will you reach?
6. Where shall I meet you?

Closing statements (examples)

1. Yeah, see you soon, Bye, Take Care
2. Bye, Take Care

3. Talk to you soon, Take Care
4. Looking forward to meet you, bye for now.
5. Likewise (when so other person says "Good to talk to you or meet you)
6. It was lovely to talk to you, bye.
7. Keep in touch, bye.

# Answers

## Worksheet (I)

1. I am a girl.
2. You are very nice.
3. Hari is a good boy
4. They are single girls.
5. We are very happy
6. This is a ball
7. These are two chairs.
8. Sonu & Preeti are good friends.
9. Mini is very helpful
10. I am five years old
11. This book is very interesting.
12. He is very tall.
13. They are reading a book.
14. It is a big elephant
15. The girls are going to the mall.

## Worksheet (II)

1. I was so happy yesterday.
2. You were very busy on Sunday.
3. Shanti & Monty were late for school yesterday.
4. She was in Delhi last month.
5. We were at school last Saturday.

6. The boys were climbing the trees.
7. He was swimming in the pool.
8. The monkey was eating the banana.
9. The dog was sleeping.
10. They were very rude.

## Worksheet (III)

1. They have an exam tomorrow.
2. An apple has many seeds.
3. My brother has many cars.
4. Dia has long hair
5. We had a lot of fun yesterday
6. She had a dog, but he died some days ago
7. Do you have a rough notebook?
8. I have a beautiful pencil box.

## Worksheet (IV)

1. I have been studying in this school since 2015.
2. I like to spend time with my dog.
3. He gave me a pen on my birthday.
4. I went to the doctor yesterday.
5. Neeraj went to Goa for summer holidays.
6. I went to the market with my family.

www.ingramcontent.com/pod-product-compliance
Ingram Content Group UK Ltd.
Pitfield, Milton Keynes, MK11 3LW, UK
UKHW041850190726
13854UKWH00002B/808

9 789357 414364